STEP INTO READING®

STEP 3

MARC BROWN

ARTHUR BREAKS THE BANK

Random House 🏠 New York

www.stepintoreading.com

Educators and librarians, for a variety of teaching tools, visit us at www.randomhouse.com/teachers

Library of Congress Cataloging-in-Publication Data
Brown, Marc Tolon.
Arthur breaks the bank / Marc Brown. — 1st ed.
p.   cm. — (Step into reading books)
SUMMARY: Arthur starts saving the money he earns in order to buy a surprise birthday present for D.W.
ISBN 0-375-81002-1 (trade) — ISBN 0-375-91002-6 (lib. bdg.)
[1. Saving and investment—Fiction. 2. Brothers and sisters—Fiction. 3. Gifts—Fiction. 4. Aardvark—Fiction.]
I. Title. II. Series: Step into reading books. Step 3.
PZ7.B81618Alc 2004 [E]—dc22 2003013586

Printed in the United States of America   First Edition   10 9 8 7 6 5 4 3 2 1

Arthur was not good
at saving money.
He liked to treat his friends
to ice cream cones . . .

and sometimes the movies.

His piggy bank

was always empty.

Then one day Arthur said,
"I'm going to start saving
my money."
He put three quarters
into his piggy bank.
Clink! Clink! Clink!
"What are you saving for?"
D.W. asked.
"It's a secret," he said.

Arthur earned money by
mowing grass . . .

raking leaves . . .

collecting bottles . . .

and walking dogs.

He put the money
in his bank on his night table.
"What are you saving for?"
asked D.W.
"You're the last person I'd tell,"
said Arthur.

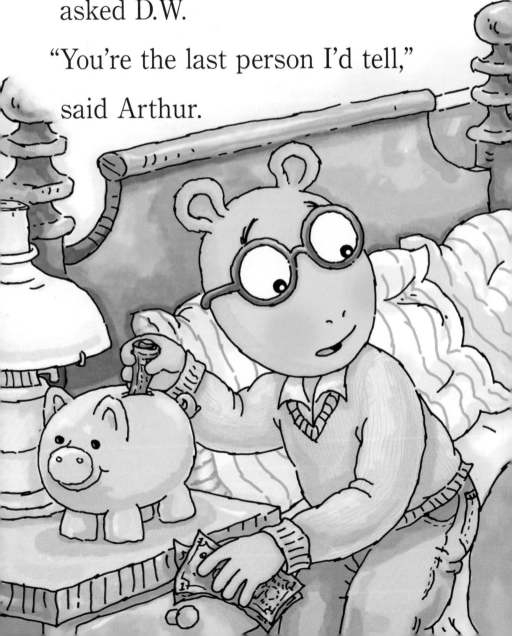

"I bet I know," she said.
"It's that Bionic Bunny game
    that Mom says is too expensive
    and will rot your brain."

"Guess again," said Arthur.

"A new baseball glove," said D.W.

"Nope," he said.

"I've got it!" she said.

"It's this scooter."

"You're not even warm," he said.

"A pony!" she said.

"A pony!" laughed Arthur.

"Where would we keep a pony?"

"The pony can stay in my room."

"I'm not saving money for a pony," said Arthur.

"What then?" she begged.

"Tell me!"

"No way," said Arthur.

After Arthur wrote his
book report, he called Buster.
"I'm going to break the bank
tomorrow," he said.
"I can't wait.
I hope I have enough money."

The next morning, Arthur woke
to a terrible surprise.
His piggy bank was not
on the night table . . .
or on his desk . . .

or on his chest of drawers . . .

or under
the bed . . .

or anywhere in his room!

"I'VE BEEN ROBBED!"

screamed Arthur.

Arthur's mom and dad
came running.
"Now I can't buy
the Mary Moo-Cow Fun Barn
for D.W.'s birthday tomorrow,"
said Arthur.
"Don't worry," said Mom.
"I think someone else
is getting her that."

Just then D.W. burst into
the room.

"You mean all your work
was for me?" she said.

She gave Arthur a hug.

20

"Don't go away," she said.

"I'll be right back."

And she ran to her room.

D.W. came back
with Arthur's piggy bank.
"Why, you little thief,"
said Arthur.
"I took it for safekeeping,"
said D.W. "I was afraid
you were going to buy
something silly."

"Now you've got
lots of money.
I sure could use all
the Mary Moo-Cow Fun Barn
accessories!" said D.W.